Cow takes a bow

Russell Punter

Illustrated by Fred Blunt

Today the circus is in town.

CIRCUS

Brown Cow sets out
to track it down.

"I'd like a seat, please,"
says Brown Cow.

Here comes the boss.
Cow sees him frown.

"I'll help," says Cow.

"Just show me how."

Cow slips and trips.

She tries some tricks...

...but drops the pies,

and spills the bricks.

Her tricycle just spins around.

Her trumpet makes a silly sound.

Her juggling balls all hit the ground.

Her hat flies off.

Her pants fall down.

Am I the biggest fool in town?

"It's all gone wrong!"
Brown Cow flops down.

Now she's the one who wears a frown.

"I'm sorry I messed up!" howls Cow.

“No, wait!”
the boss shouts.

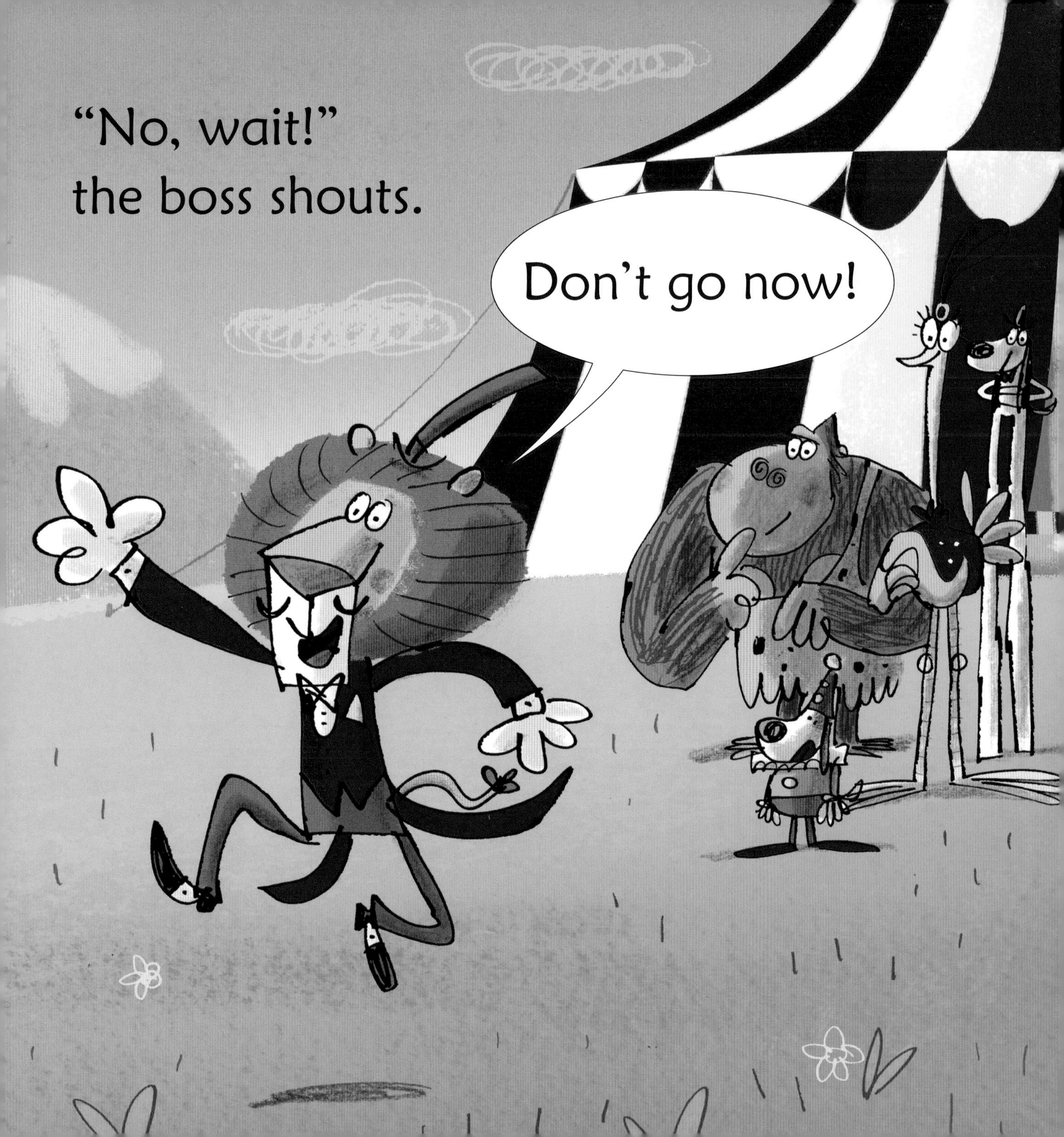

"Listen!" he says.

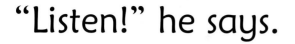

The crowd shouts, "Wow!"

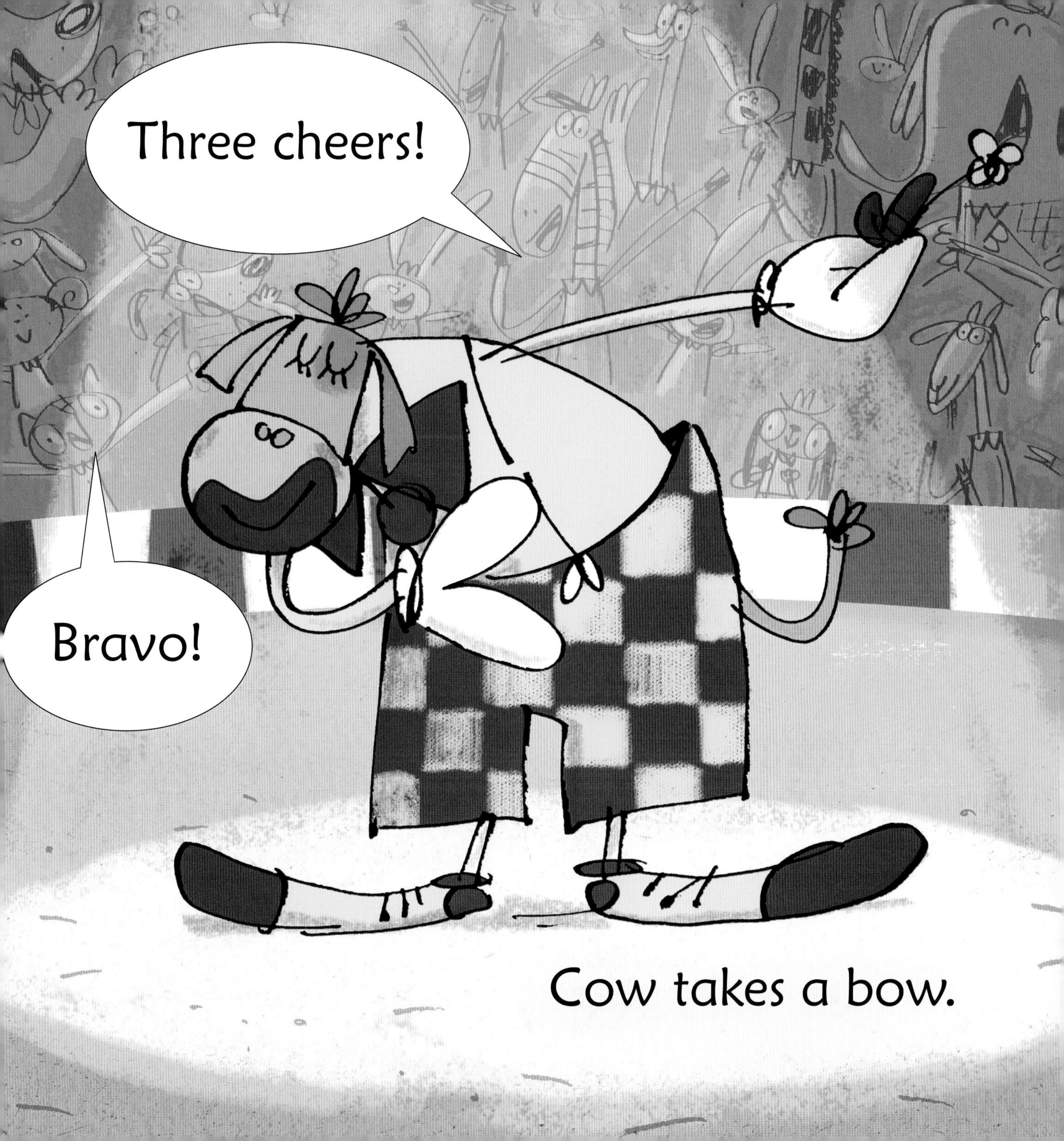

Cow takes a bow.

About phonics

Phonics is a method of teaching reading which is used extensively in today's schools. At its heart is an emphasis on identifying the *sounds* of letters, or combinations of letters, that are then put together to make words. These sounds are known as phonemes.

Starting to read
Learning to read is an important milestone for any child. The process can begin well before children start to learn letters and put them together to read words. The sooner children can discover books and enjoy stories and language, the better they will be prepared for reading themselves, first with the help of an adult and then independently.

You can find out more about phonics on the Usborne Very First Reading website, **www.usborne.com/veryfirstreading** (US readers go to **www.veryfirstreading.com**). Click on the **Parents** tab at the top of the page, then scroll down and click on **About synthetic phonics**.

Phonemic awareness

An important early stage in pre-reading and early reading is developing phonemic awareness: that is, listening out for the sounds within words. Rhymes, rhyming stories and alliteration are excellent ways of encouraging phonemic awareness.

In this story, your child will soon identify the *ow* sound, as in **Brown Cow** or in **around** or **ground**. Look out, too, for rhymes such as **today** – **hooray** and **slips** – **trips**.

Hearing your child read

If your child is reading a story to you, don't rush to correct mistakes, but be ready to prompt or guide if he or she is struggling. Above all, do give plenty of praise and encouragement.

Edited by Jenny Tyler, Lesley Sims and Mairi Mackinnon

Designed by Caroline Spatz

First published in 2013 by Usborne Publishing Ltd., Usborne House, 83-85 Saffron Hill, London EC1N 8RT, England.
www.usborne.com Copyright © 2013 Usborne Publishing Ltd.